SOMEDAY RIDER

By Ann Herbert Scott
Illustrated by Ronald Himler

Clarion Books

New York

Clarion Books
a Houghton Mifflin Company imprint
52 Vanderbilt Avenue, New York, NY 10017
Text copyright © 1989 by Ann Herbert Scott
Illustrations copyright © 1989 by Ronald Himler

Library of Congress Cataloging-in-Publication Data
Scott, Ann Herbert.
Someday rider / by Ann Herbert Scott; illustrated by Ronald
Himler.
p.   cm.
Summary: Kenny longs to be a cowboy like his father and the others,
and finally his sympathetic mother teaches him how to
ride.
ISBN 0-89919-792-2
[1. Cowboys—Fiction.]   I. Himler, Ronald, ill.   II. Title.
PZ7.S415So   1989
[E]—dc19   88-35255
CIP
AC

Y 10 9 8 7 6 5 4 3 2 1

For the Bakers of Mountain City
and the Badgers of Elko
Ted, Betty, Frank, Della, Sharon, Mike, Beau and Brett—
the best of riders
and the best of friends

— A.H.S.

Every morning before sunrise Kenny ran down to the corral to watch his father and the other cowboys begin the day's work.

First the cowboys caught their horses. Then they bridled and saddled them. And then as the sun climbed over the mountain, they rode off to the far hills.

Every morning Kenny carefully fastened the gate
behind the riders and waved good-bye from his seat on
the top rail of the corral.

When they remembered, his father and the other
cowboys turned in their saddles and waved back.

"Someday you'll ride with those big cowboys,"
Kenny's mother told him one morning as she rinsed the
milk can in the sink.

"Someday! Someday!" Kenny shook his head. "I'm
tired of somedays. I don't want to be a someday rider.
I want to ride right now."

"Someday when you're bigger."

"I'm big right now," said Kenny.

"Yes, you are," said his mother. "You're big enough
to churn this butter all by yourself."

Round and round Kenny turned the handle of the butter churn. As he turned, he thought of the cowboys off in the hills. Suddenly he had an idea. As soon as the butter came in clumps, he ran to the chicken yard where Mrs. Agnes Goose was scratching for an early lunch.

"Hi, there, Mrs. Goose," called Kenny.

"Honk," answered Mrs. Agnes Goose.

"How about a ride?" asked Kenny. Then, without waiting for an answer, he climbed on her back.

"Honk, honk, honk!" screamed Mrs. Goose, flapping her great wings and dumping Kenny in the mud.

Before breakfast the next morning, Kenny hurried down the lane toward the corral. Under his boots the grass was wet. Over his head the stars were bright and near.

Kenny sang to himself. His voice was loud enough so the horses would hear and not be afraid, just the way cowboys sing as they ride night herd on the cattle.

"Well, good morning, Cowboy Kenny."

Kenny jumped. It was his father, carrying a sack of grain from the barn.

"Good morning, Dad."

"And how's Cowboy Kenny this morning?"

"Terrible."

"What's the trouble?"

"I'm tired of staying home with Mom. I want to ride with you and the other cowboys. Please, Dad, please take me along."

"Someday," his father told him. "But for right now, how about helping me take this grain down to the corral."

After the cowboys rode off that morning, Kenny headed for the upper pasture where his dad kept the sheep.

"Hi there, Amelia," he called to the biggest, fattest sheep.

"Baaaaah," Amelia answered.

Kenny climbed on a nearby rock. "How about a ride?" he asked Amelia.

Up in the air Amelia bolted. Crash—down came Kenny, right in the middle of a thistle bush.

By the time Kenny took out the worst prickles, Amelia had moved to the far end of the pasture. "You're not much of a horse anyway," Kenny shouted as he started for home.

The next morning Kenny brought in one load of firewood after another for the kitchen stove. After his work was done, he headed for the lower pasture where the mother cows were grazing with their calves.

"Mooo," one mother cow bellowed at Kenny.

"Mooo to you," Kenny answered.

There were so many cows and calves it was hard to choose. Then Kenny saw a little calf playing alone by the side of the stream. The calf stopped playing to look at him.

"Here I come," Kenny cried, throwing his arms around the little calf's neck.

Up in the air the calf bounded. Splash—down came Kenny right in the middle of the stream.

Kenny rubbed his eyes and tried not to cry.

"Who'd want you for a horse?" he yelled as he grabbed
a willow branch and pulled himself from the stream.

The calf ran off to find its mother. Kenny looked
toward the kitchen window, hoping his own mother
wasn't watching. Quickly he dumped the water from his
boots and sloshed back to the house. *Maybe she won't even
notice,* he thought to himself as he changed into a clean
shirt and jeans.

In the kitchen Kenny's mother was taking pies from the oven. "Kenneth," she called, "I want to speak to you."

Kenny stuffed his wet jeans under his bed and hurried to the kitchen. "Yes, Mom," he said.

"Son, I think it's finally time."

"Time for what, Mom?"

"Time for you to start real riding. You've waited long enough."

"You mean right now?" Kenny asked.

"Right now," said his mother, hanging her apron on the hook by the sink.

At the barn Kenny's mother lifted her old saddle onto Sagebrush, the horse she had ridden when she was a girl. "Sagebrush is a good little cow horse, Kenneth. Many's the time we helped my dad with the roundup when I wasn't much bigger than you are now."

Kenny climbed into the saddle. He liked the feel of sitting there alone, high above the ground. "Mom," he said, "let's keep it a secret."

"Let's," said his mother as she adjusted his stirrups. "We'll wait for the right time to tell Dad."

So they did. Every morning after the work was
done, Kenny and his mother went down to the corral
to practice riding. Every afternoon before the cowboys

came home, Kenny and Sagebrush helped herd the milk cows back to the barn. And every night, fast asleep in bed, Kenny galloped off to the far hills in his dreams.

At last the right time came. Kenny's father was in the kitchen drinking a second cup of coffee.

"You look worried," his mother said.

"I am, a little," said his father. "We're rounding up cattle for branding tomorrow and we sure are short of hands. I'd counted on the Mitchell boys coming up from town, but they're both busy."

"Dad," said Kenny, "I know where there's another hand."

His mother winked at Kenny. "As a matter of fact, I know where there are two hands," she said.

Then Kenny and his mother and father walked down to the corral together.

The next morning everyone—Kenny's father and his
mother and the other cowboys and Kenny himself—rode
off together for the roundup.

Kenny turned in his saddle. He waved good-bye to
Mrs. Agnes Goose and the chickens, Amelia and the
sheep, and the calves grazing with their mothers in the
lower pasture.

Kenny gave Sagebrush a quick pat. "You're a good horse," he told him, "the best horse I ever rode. And someday really is today."

Then Kenny and Sagebrush joined the other riders on the trail to the far hills.

JC

Scott, Ann Herbert

Someday rider

DATE DUE
